LILLY'S PURPLE PLASTIC PURSE

BY KEVIN HENKES

GREENWILLOW BOOKS, NEW YORK

For Will

Lilly's Purple Plastic Purse
Copyright © 1996 by Kevin Henkes
All rights reserved.
Manufactured in China by South China Printing Company Ltd.
For information address HarperCollins Children's Books,
a division of HarperCollins Publishers,
195 Broadway, New York, NY 10007.
www.harperchildrens.com

Watercolor paints and a black pen were used for the full-color art.
The text type is Veljovic.

Library of Congress Cataloging-in-Publication Data
Henkes, Kevin.
Lilly's purple plastic purse / by Kevin Henkes.
    p.   cm.
Summary: Lilly loves everything about school, especially her teacher, but
when he asks her to wait a while before showing her new purse, she does
something for which she is very sorry later.
ISBN 0-688-12897-1 (trade).   ISBN 0-688-12898-X (lib. bdg.)
[1. Schools—Fiction. 2. Teachers—Fiction.] I. Title.
PZ7.H389Li   1996   [E]—dc20   95-25085   CIP   AC

First Edition   14 15 16 SCP 30 29 28

 Greenwillow Books

I LOVE SCHOOL!

LILLY loved school.

She loved the pointy pencils.

She loved the squeaky chalk.

And she loved the way her boots
went clickety-clickety-click
down the long, shiny hallways.

MINE!

Lilly loved the privacy
of her very own desk.

She loved the fish sticks
and chocolate milk
every Friday
in the lunchroom.

STRAWS MAKE EVERYTHING
TASTE
BETTER!

FOR YOU!

And, most of all,
she loved her teacher,
Mr. Slinger.

Mr. Slinger was as sharp as a tack.

He wore artistic shirts.

He wore glasses on a chain around his neck.

And he wore a different colored tie

for each day of the week.

"Wow," said Lilly. That was just about all she could say. "Wow."

Instead of "Greetings, students"
or "Good morning, pupils,"
Mr. Slinger winked and said, "Howdy!"

He thought that desks in rows
were old-fashioned and boring.
"Do you rodents think you
can handle a semicircle?"

And he always provided
the most tasty snacks—
things that were curly
and crunchy and cheesy.

"I want to be a teacher
when I grow up," said Lilly.
"Me, too!" said her friends
Chester and Wilson and Victor.

At home Lilly pretended to be Mr. Slinger.

"I am the teacher," she told her baby brother, Julius. "Listen up!"

Lilly even wanted her own set of deluxe picture encyclopedias.

"What's with Lilly?" asked her mother.

"I thought she wanted to be a surgeon or an ambulance driver
or a diva," said her father.

"It must be because of her new teacher, Mr. Slinger," said her mother.

"Wow," said her father. That was just about all he could say. "Wow."

Whenever the students had free time, they were permitted to go
to the Lightbulb Lab in the back of the classroom.

They expressed their ideas creatively through drawing and writing.

Lilly went often.

She had a *lot* of ideas.

She drew pictures of Mr. Slinger.

And she wrote stories about him, too.

During Sharing Time, Lilly showed her creations to the entire class.

"Wow," said Mr. Slinger. That was just about all he could say. "Wow."

BIG FRIENDLY
MR. NICE MAN
TEACHER!
by me Lilly

AND AT THE
VERY LAST SECOND
MR. SLINGER
SAVED THE COLD,
STARVING,
ELDERLY...

When Mr. Slinger had bus duty,
Lilly stood in line even though
she didn't ride the bus.

CALL ON ME!
PLEASE!
PLEASE!

Lilly raised her hand
more than anyone else in class
(even if she didn't know the answer).

And she volunteered to stay
after school to clap erasers.

"I want to be a teacher
when I grow up," said Lilly.
"Excellent choice," said Mr. Slinger.

One Monday morning Lilly came to school especially happy.
She had gone shopping with her Grammy over the weekend.
Lilly had a new pair of movie star sunglasses, complete with
glittery diamonds and a chain like Mr. Slinger's.
She had three shiny quarters.
And, best of all, she had a brand new purple plastic purse
that played a jaunty tune when it was opened.

Lilly wanted to show everyone.
"Not now," said Mr. Slinger.
"Listen to our story."
Lilly had a hard time listening.

Lilly *really* wanted to show everyone.
"Not now," said Mr. Slinger.
"Let's be considerate of our classmates."
Lilly had a hard time being considerate.

Lilly *really, really* wanted to show everyone.
"Not now," said Mr. Slinger.
"Wait until recess or Sharing Time."
But Lilly could not wait.

The glasses were so glittery.
The quarters were so shiny.
And the purse played such
nice music, not to mention
how excellent it was for
storing school supplies.

"Look," Lilly whispered fiercely.
"Look, everyone. Look what I've got!"
Everyone looked.
Including Mr. Slinger.
He was not amused.

"I'll just keep your things at my desk
until the end of the day," said
Mr. Slinger. "They'll be safe there,
and then you can take them home."

Lilly's stomach lurched.
She felt like crying.
Her glasses were gone.
Her quarters were gone.
Her purple plastic purse was gone.
Lilly longed for her purse all morning.
She was even too sad to eat the snack
Mr. Slinger served before recess.

That afternoon Lilly went to the Lightbulb Lab.

She was still very sad.

She thought and she thought and she thought.

And then she became angry.

She thought and she thought and she thought some more.

And then she became furious.

She thought and she thought and she thought a bit longer.

And then she drew a picture of Mr. Slinger.

Right before the last bell rang, Lilly sneaked the drawing
into Mr. Slinger's book bag.

When all the students were buttoned and zipped and snapped
and tied and ready to go home, Mr. Slinger strolled over to
Lilly and gave her purple plastic purse back.

"It's a beautiful purse," said Mr. Slinger. "Your quarters are nice
and jingly. And those glasses are absolutely fabulous. You may
bring them back to school as long as you don't disturb the rest
of the class."

"I do not want to be a teacher when I grow up," Lilly said
as she marched out of the classroom.

On the way home Lilly opened her purse.
Her glasses and quarters were inside.
And so was a note from Mr. Slinger. It said:
　　"Today was a difficult day.
　　Tomorrow will be better."
There was also a small bag of tasty snacks
at the bottom of the purse.

Lilly's stomach lurched.
She felt like crying.
She felt simply awful.

Lilly ran all the way home and told her mother and father everything.

Instead of watching her favorite cartoons, Lilly decided
to sit in the uncooperative chair.

I'LL STAY
HERE A
MILLION
YEARS FOR
MR. SLINGER.

WHY DOES
EVERYTHING
ALWAYS HAPPEN
TO ME?

ONE THOUSAND FIFTY-ONE,
ONE THOUSAND
FIFTY-TWO,
ONE THOUSAND
NINETY-NINE...

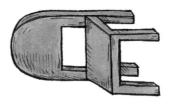

That night Lilly drew a new picture of Mr. Slinger
and wrote a story about him, too.

Lilly's mother wrote a note.
And Lilly's father baked some tasty snacks for Lilly to take
to school the next day.
"I think Mr. Slinger will understand," said Lilly's mother.
"I know he will," said Lilly's father.

The next morning Lilly got to school early.

"These are for you," Lilly said to Mr. Slinger.

"Because I'm really, really, really, really, really, really, really, really, really, really, really, really, really, really, really, really, really, really, really sorry."

Mr. Slinger read the story.

And he looked at the picture.

And he read the note.

And he sampled the snacks.

"Wow," said Mr. Slinger. That was just about all he could say. "Wow."

"What do you think we should do with this?" asked Mr. Slinger.

"Could we just throw it away?" asked Lilly.

"Excellent idea," said Mr. Slinger.

During Sharing Time, Lilly demonstrated the many uses and unique qualities of her purple plastic purse, her shiny quarters, and her glittery movie star sunglasses.

Then she did a little performance using them as props.

"It's called Interpretive Dance," said Lilly.

Mr. Slinger joined in.

"Wow," said the entire class. That was just about all they could say. "Wow."

Throughout the rest of the day, Lilly's purse and quarters
and sunglasses were tucked safely inside her desk.
She peeked at them often but did not disturb a soul.

Right before the last bell rang, Mr. Slinger served Lilly's snacks,
to everyone's delight.

"What do you want to be when you grow up?" asked Mr. Slinger.

"A TEACHER!" everyone responded. Lilly's response was
the loudest.

"Excellent choice," said Mr. Slinger.

As the pupils filed out of the classroom,
Lilly held her purple plastic purse close to her heart.
Mr. Slinger was right—it *had* been a better day.

Lilly ran and skipped and hopped and flew all the way home,
she was so happy.
And she really *did* want to be a teacher when she grew up—

That is, when she didn't want to be a dancer
or a surgeon or an ambulance driver or a diva
or a pilot or a hairdresser or a scuba diver . . .